BRYCE CANYON
NATIONAL

Danger in the Narrows

Mike Graf

Illustrated by
Marjorie Leggitt

Adventures with the Parkers

FALCON GUIDES

GUILFORD, CONNECTICUT
HELENA, MONTANA
AN IMPRINT OF GLOBE PEQUOT PRESS

FALCON**GUIDES**®

Text © 2006, 2012 Mike Graf
Illustrations © 2006, 2012 Marjorie Leggitt

FalconGuides is an imprint of Globe Pequot Press.
Falcon, FalconGuides, and Outfit Your Mind are registered trademarks of Morris Book Publishing, LLC.

Maps courtesy of the National Park Service

Photo credits:
Licensed by Shutterstock.com: 1: © kavram; 5: © John Vanhara; 6: © Christina Tisi-Kramer; 7: © Joel Baucat Grant; 10–11: © John Vanhara; 13: © sigurcamp; 14: © Kushch Dmitry; 17 (top): © Andre St-Louis; 17 (bottom): © Jennifer Leigh Selig; 19: © Laura Theis; 22: © atm2003; page 24: shooarts; page 26 (top): © Michael Thompson; page 26 (center): © John Vanhara; 26 (bottom): © Michael Thompson; 27 (top): © dibrova; 27 (bottom): © Christina Tisi-Kramer; 29: © alvsta; 30: © Joel Baucat Grant; 31 (top and bottom right) © John Vanhara; 31 (bottom left): © richsantaclaus; 33: © James M. Phelps Jr.; 34: © Jason Buss; 35: unknown; 37: © Krzysztof Wiktor; 38 (left): © kompasstudio; 38 (right): © Edward Hardam; 40: © John Vanhara; 41: unknown (2), Vivian Fung (left); Krzysztof Wiktor (right); 42: © Aspen Photo, Logan Carter, Peter Wey; page 44: unknown; page 47: © Nickolay Stanev, Chris Geszvain, Jim Lopes; 50: © Nickolay Stanev; 53: © Rudy Balasko; 54: © Krzysztof Wiktor; 55: © Galyna Andrushko; 57: © Krzysztof Wiktor; 59: © Krzysztof Wiktor; 62: © Jason Maehl; 63: © Linda Armstrong; 65: Rick Laverty; 66: © Julie Flavin Photography; 67: © Dean Pennala; 69: unknown; 70: © Dean Pennala; 71: © Jim Lopes; 77: © Linda Armstrong; 78: unknown; 79: © Stacy Funderburke; 85: © Terry Reimink; 86: © Alexey Kamenskiy; 87 (left): © James M Phelps, Jr.; 87 (right): unknown; 90 (left): © Joel Bauchat Grant; 90 (right): © Krzysztof Wiktor; 91: © Michael Thompson; 92 (left): © Chee-Onn Leong; 92 (right): © Mariia Sats; 93: © James M. Pelps, Jr.; 94: © Andrzej Gibasiewicz
Courtesy of NASA: 23
Courtesy of National Park Service: 39

Illustrations: Marjorie Leggitt
Models for the twins: Amanda and Benjamin Frazier

Project editor: David Legere

Library of Congress Cataloging-in-Publication Data is available on file.

ISBN 978-0-7627-7974-1

Printed in the United States of America

10 9 8 7 6 5 4 3 2 1

"Got everything packed?" James's mom called from down the hall. "I think so, Mom," James answered.

"How about you, Morgan?" Mom asked.

"I'm all set to go," Morgan said. "I'm packing my camera right now. Are you and Dad ready?"

"Almost," Mom said. "Your father is putting all the camping gear in the car. I've got the cooler. And that should do it."

"I'm all packed," James called out. He folded up his map of the southwestern United States, slipped it into his daypack, and carried the pack out to the car.

Morgan slung her duffel bag over her shoulder. She stopped at her door and looked back. "Good-bye, bedroom. I'll see you in a few weeks."

While her parents finished packing, Morgan sat down, pulled out her journal, and wrote.

Monday, July 17, 4 a.m.

Dear Diary,

I'm really looking forward to this vacation. My parents, my brother James, and I have been planning it for months. We've never been to a national park before, and the searches I've done on the Internet make it seem like Bryce and Zion are perfect for us. I can't wait to do some of the hikes my parents have been telling us about. You see, my parents met in Zion while they were in college. So this, for them, is sort of an anniversary. But for my twin brother James and me, it's a whole new thing. And I can't wait!

More later.

Hasta la vista,

Morgan

James was studying the road map.

Dad glanced over at him while driving. "We've been on the road ten hours already. How much farther do we have?"

"We should be hitting the turnoff soon," James answered. "From there, it should only be an hour or so more."

Dad smiled. "Only?" He looked in the rearview mirror. His wife, Kristen, was asleep in the backseat. Morgan was leaning over. Her head rested on her mother's shoulder.

"Are you excited?" Dad asked James.

"Yep," James answered. "You and Mom have been talking about this for so long. I can't wait to see all the rock formations."

"Me too," Dad said. "Twenty years is a long time."

James folded up the map and pulled out his journal.

Monday, July 17, 2 p.m.

This is James Parker reporting.

Our vacation has started. We are right now in the middle of a long drive to Bryce Canyon and Zion National Parks.

Dad has been talking about this "back to nature" trip for years. He says he's been waiting until Morgan and I were old enough to really experience the wilderness. I guess at ten years old, we finally are.

And, boy, are we going to experience things. We've got water filters, backpacks, water bottles, power bars, tents, and tiny backpacking stoves. Mom and Dad say we're going to be hiking all over the place!

After spending two weeks at outdoor camp this summer, I know I'm ready. I hope my family can keep up with me!

I will be writing more soon.

James

"Are you going to write in your journal, Dad?" Morgan asked while sitting up and stretching.

"Of course. We all agreed on that," Dad answered. "Maybe when your mom takes over driving."

"You'll have to wait until I wake up," Mom mumbled from the backseat.

"How about in a few minutes?" Dad asked.

"That will give me a moment to write now," Mom said. She pulled out her journal.

Monday, July 17, 3 p.m.
Dear Diary,
It's been a long time since I've written in a journal, but I'm glad I am. I can't wait to take the twins to Bryce and Zion. It was twenty years ago there that I met my husband, Robert. And it seems like yesterday. But I know a lot has changed since then. I studied biology while in college, and that was part of my job as a ranger when I worked at Zion. I'm still interested in the park wildlife. I wonder if there are any endangered species now and if any plants or animals have been reintroduced in the parks. It will be interesting to find out!
Sincerely,
Kristen

At the junction, Dad pulled over. The family climbed out.

"Anybody need anything?" Dad asked. "There's a store here."

"Nope," the rest of the family chimed in.

"Well, let's go!" Mom said. She walked around to the other side of the car and slid into the driver's seat.

Morgan climbed into the passenger seat beside her.

"See those red cliffs up ahead?" Dad asked. "If I remember correctly, that's Red Canyon. It's a lot like Bryce. That's where the drive really gets interesting. The park isn't far past that."

"Cool! Only a few more minutes till we get there," James exclaimed.

Dad pulled out his journal.

Monday, July 17, 3:15 p.m.

Hi! This is Robert Parker writing. I'm finally going back to Bryce and Zion, two of the most unique places in the world. I wonder if any of the rock formations have changed—would I even know? When I was in college, I studied geology. In the summer, I worked at Zion where I got to see some of the most interesting geology in the world. Now I get to share this place with my two kids. I can't wait to hike all the trails. I remember many of them: Peekaboo, Angels Landing, Emerald Pools, and the Narrows. This is going to be great!

Robert Parker

"Here's the turnoff to the park," Mom said. She turned right.

"Only three miles to go!" James announced.

"This is exciting!" Dad said, while looking out the window. "We're finally here. And I'm sharing this with my three favorite people in the world."

Red Canyon tunnel

Within a few minutes, they reached the park entrance sign.

"Let's get out and take a picture," Morgan suggested.

"Good idea," Mom said. She pulled over to the side of the road.

The family hopped out of the car and walked toward the sign.

Morgan watched a woman take a photo. "Would you please take our picture?" Morgan asked her.

"Sure," she replied.

"Great!" Morgan said. She gave the woman her camera and joined her family next to the sign.

"Say 'cheese!'"

"Cheese!"

SNAP! The woman took the picture.

"Come on," Dad said. "We've got just enough time to do a hike."

"Great." James said. "Let's go!"

The family drove up to the entrance station. Dad got out his Intra-agency Annual Pass and showed it to the ranger. The ranger handed them a park map and newspaper, and they drove into the park.

View into Bryce Canyon—wow!

"We're going hiking down there?" Morgan asked.

The family stood at an overlook at Bryce Point. Below them was the entire canyon. It was an amazing view of colorful, bizarrely shaped rocks.

"The trail starts here," James pointed out. "It's a mile down, then a three-mile loop on the Peekaboo Trail."

They hiked down switchbacks. As soon as they were in the canyon, they were surrounded by tall pinnacles of red and orange rock.

"They're called hoodoos," James said, looking at the rock towers.

"This whole area looks like Fantasyland at Disneyland," Mom said.

"Yeah, and every turn in the trail leads us to a whole bunch of unreal formations," Dad said. "I wonder what Ebenezer Bryce thought when he first hiked out here."

NAMESAKE

Ebenezer Bryce was a farmer who lived in a cabin near Tropic, the town below the park. He came to the area in 1875 to harvest timber. He also herded cattle in the canyon. Even though Bryce only lived there for five years, the park was at first called Bryce's Canyon and then later Bryce's National Monument. After that, it was called Utah National Park, but that name didn't stick. The name was later changed back to Bryce Canyon National Park.

"It sure is quite a maze of rocks," Mom added.

The family walked on, admiring the scenery. They soon came to another bend in the trail. Ahead of them was a tunnel carved out of the rock. James and Morgan ran through the tunnel and out the other side. Quickly, they hid behind a rock wall.

"Boo!" they jumped out and shouted, just as their parents arrived.

"Somehow I knew that was going to happen," Dad said, smiling.

"No wonder they call this the Peekaboo Trail," Mom said. "Look up. See those windows in the rocks?"

"Hey—let me take everyone's picture," Morgan suggested.

The family gathered together. Morgan stepped back. "There. Perfect," she said. "Hold still."

Morgan took the picture. "It's going to be quite a slide show."

"And we can e-mail all the pictures to our relatives too," James added.

The family hiked farther along. Morgan kept taking pictures.

Mom stopped next to a tall tree. "It's a ponderosa pine. Smell the bark."

"Mmm," Morgan said. "It smells so sweet."

"Like vanilla," James added.

"Or butterscotch," Dad said. "I wish we could bottle that smell and take it home."

"It makes me hungry," James said, pulling an energy bar from his backpack.

They walked on.

"You know," Dad thought out loud, "these rock pinnacles look like different objects. I remember rock formations in the park with names like Hat Shop, Thor's Hammer, and Tower Bridge. I wonder if we'll see anything like that here."

"That one looks like shark fins," James said, pointing ahead.

"Or stegosaurus plates," added Morgan.

Later, Mom passed by an oddly shaped hoodoo. "This one looks like a gargoyle."

"Or maybe a gnome," Dad said.

"I think the whole area looks like a giant sand castle at the beach," James announced. "Only a wave of water has washed over it and it's half melted."

"You mean eroded," Dad said. "These rocks have been weathered by water."

HOW THE HOODOO GREW

Long ago, this area of Utah was a large freshwater lake. Minerals got into the sedimentary rock, and that gave the rocks color. When the water dried up, the layer of rock was left behind. Later, the area uplifted as part of a region called the Colorado Plateau. But the hoodoos we see now are created in three steps:

1. Nights are cold at Bryce. More than 200 days a year have freezing nights with thawing days. When this happens, water from rain and snow melts and seeps into the joints, or cracks, of the rocks. Freezing water expands, breaking apart areas of weak rock.

2. Rainwater, which naturally has acid in it, dissolves limestone. This further erodes the rocks at Bryce.

3. Gullies of water run down slopes from Bryce's rim. This helps to cut deep, narrow walls called fins. Fins get holes in them, which are called windows. Windows grow larger until they collapse, creating hoodoos. As old hoodoos collapse, new ones are formed.

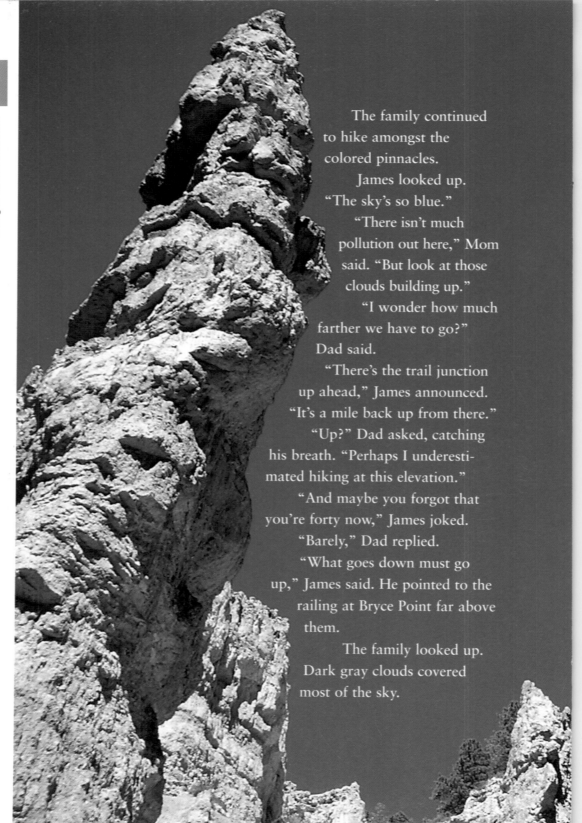

The family continued to hike amongst the colored pinnacles.

James looked up. "The sky's so blue."

"There isn't much pollution out here," Mom said. "But look at those clouds building up."

"I wonder how much farther we have to go?" Dad said.

"There's the trail junction up ahead," James announced. "It's a mile back up from there."

"Up?" Dad asked, catching his breath. "Perhaps I underestimated hiking at this elevation."

"And maybe you forgot that you're forty now," James joked.

"Barely," Dad replied.

"What goes down must go up," James said. He pointed to the railing at Bryce Point far above them.

The family looked up. Dark gray clouds covered most of the sky.

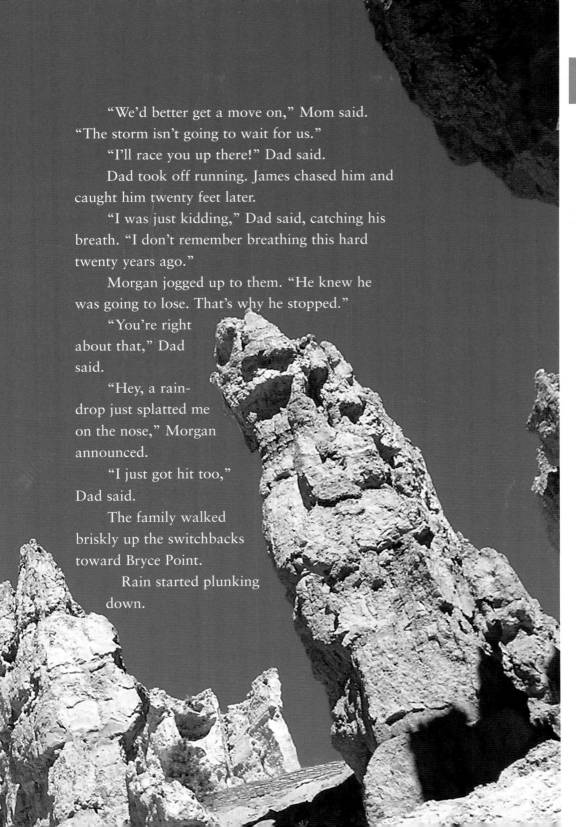

"We'd better get a move on," Mom said. "The storm isn't going to wait for us."

"I'll race you up there!" Dad said.

Dad took off running. James chased him and caught him twenty feet later.

"I was just kidding," Dad said, catching his breath. "I don't remember breathing this hard twenty years ago."

Morgan jogged up to them. "He knew he was going to lose. That's why he stopped."

"You're right about that," Dad said.

"Hey, a raindrop just splatted me on the nose," Morgan announced.

"I just got hit too," Dad said.

The family walked briskly up the switchbacks toward Bryce Point.

Rain started plunking down.

The family stopped to pull their windbreakers out. As they were putting them on, the storm let go.

Tiny white balls mixed with rain hit the ground and quickly melted. "It's hailing too," James said. A few rumbles of thunder roared in the distance.

"There are only a few more switchbacks to go," Mom said.

"There's no real place to take cover anyway," Dad called out. "Let's hurry to the car."

"I'm getting cold," James said.

"And soaked," Mom added.

The hail stopped, but the rain continued. Small gullies of water washed down the sides of the trail.

"I can see my breath!" James said.

"I bet the temperature has dropped twenty degrees," Mom said.

"Okay. It looks like it's just one more switchback up," Dad called out. "And we need to not be out in the open like this. Any time thunder occurs within thirty seconds after lightning, it's time to seek shelter."

The family dashed up the last hundred feet of the trail. They reached the parking lot and ran toward their car.

James and Morgan got to the car first and jumped in. Mom and Dad were right behind.

Mom got into the driver's seat and started the car. She turned on the windshield wipers.

"Hey! The rain almost stopped," Dad said.

Morgan wiped her fogged-up window with her sleeve and looked out. "And the sun's coming out!"

Steam was rising off the parking lot pavement.

James rolled down his window. "Look, a rainbow!"

"A good sign," said Mom. "I think the storm is over."

"I'm glad," Dad said. "So let's head over to our campsite, get into dry clothes, and set up."

Dad poured pancake batter onto a frying pan on the camp stove. "Shall I wake up the kids?" he asked.

"We're not asleep," Morgan shouted from her tent.

"Yes we are!" James said from his tent.

Morgan and James climbed out of their tents and joined their parents by the picnic table.

"Are you hungry?" Dad asked the twins.

"You bet," Morgan answered.

"Me too," James said.

Dad flipped over a pancake. "These will be ready in a minute. But before you eat, why don't you walk over there?" He nodded toward a trail.

James and Morgan walked where Dad pointed. They stopped and stood at the edge of the canyon. They saw hundreds of hoodoos of all shapes, sizes, and colors.

"I can't believe we camped right next to this," Morgan said.

James and Morgan walked back to their campsite.

"We reserved this spot just for that view," Mom said. "But breakfast is ready. Why don't you two go wash your hands?"

James and Morgan grabbed soap and towels and headed over to the washroom.

After breakfast, James unfolded his park map. "Are we going to do the big hike today?" he asked.

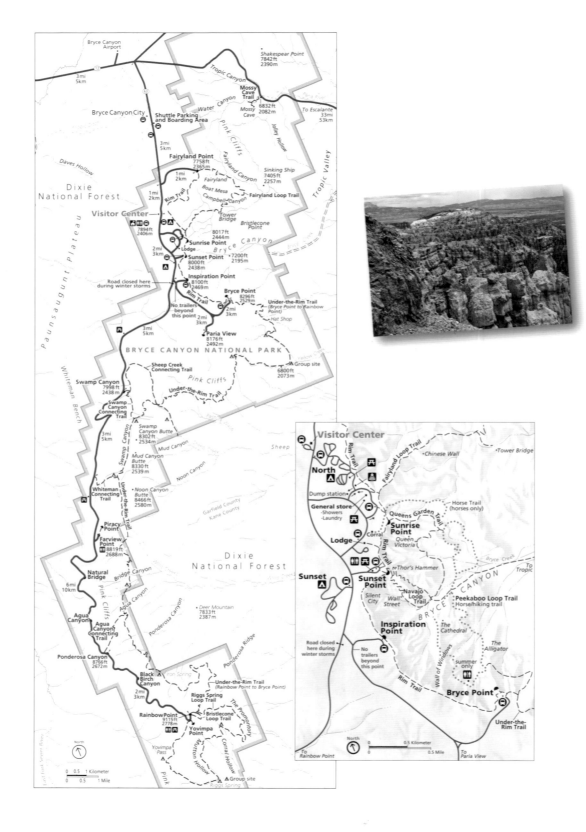

"Yes," Mom answered. "The one we've been talking about."

James studied the map. "If we hike along the rim from here, we'll get to the Queen's Garden Trail at Sunrise Point. We can go down there and hike the Navajo Loop Trail up to Wall Street."

"Sounds like a plan," Dad said, looking at James's map.

The family got ready for their hike. They put on sunscreen, sunglasses, and hats to protect their faces from the sun. Then they took off, right from their campsite.

Morgan hustled up the trail. "Let's go!"

"Bryce Canyon, here we come," James said, following her.

Mom and Dad trailed behind.

The family walked along the rim trail. To the right was a forest. To the left were views into Bryce Canyon.

"The queen awaits down below!" Morgan announced at the trail junction.

"And I wonder what else," James said.

They hiked down the switchbacks into Bryce Canyon.

Dad looked at the rock formations. "These are better than yesterday's!"

"Maybe so," Mom said. "Or maybe it's just that they're new or different."

Morgan pointed to a slanted plateau of rock in the distance. "Hey, look!"

"That's probably the Sinking Ship," James said. "It's right here on the map."

The family walked farther along.

James pointed toward a hoodoo. "I think I see a rhinoceros!"

"That could be an alien with a hat!" Morgan said.

"But over there—that looks like Snoopy," Mom said.

"I think Snow White and the Seven Dwarfs will be coming out of one of those tunnels soon," Dad said.

Mom started singing, "Hi-ho. Hi-ho. It's down the trail we go."

Dad chimed in, "Hi-ho. Hi-ho."

"Come on," Morgan said to James. "Let's keep moving before their voices cause a rock slide."

The twins disappeared around a corner. But then they quickly ran back to their parents.

James spoke in a dignified voice: "Sir, madam, the queen requests your presence. Please follow us."

James and Morgan marched ahead like guards. Their parents followed. They came to a junction in the trail. A sign read QUEEN'S GARDEN, END OF TRAIL. An arrow pointed the way.

James and Morgan led their parents up a short trail.

"The queen would like you to join her in the garden for midmorning tea," Morgan announced.

"Where's the queen?" Mom asked, looking around.

Morgan pointed to a pillar of rock. "Right up there." At the end of a group of rocks was a hoodoo shaped like a queen overlooking her garden.

"Amazing," Dad said. "Thousands of years of erosion, and we end up with a queen right here!"

"Shall we join the queen for some snacks?" Mom asked with a British accent.

"Excellent idea," James replied. "The queen has already set out chairs for you so we can sit and enjoy the view."

The family sat down on some fallen logs. They passed around fruit, crackers, and peanut butter.

"Some fine tea and crumpets we're having, old chap," Dad said to James.

"Nothing but the best from the queen," James said. He started laughing.

"Well, it's time to say good-bye to her majesty," Dad said. "We've got a ways to go to the Navajo Trail."

The family hiked out of the Queen's Garden area and back toward the main trail. They turned right and walked near a dry streambed at the canyon bottom.

"Look at those bristlecone pines on the hillside," Mom said. "I can't believe it. Right here in Bryce Canyon. They're some of the oldest living things on Earth."

The family looked at the trees. They had small, crooked trunks, and their needles were shaped like bottle brushes.

"How old are those trees?" Morgan asked.

"Some bristlecones can live to be thousands of years old," Mom said. "But those trees are probably much younger."

OLDEST IN THE WORLD

Bristlecone pine trees grow high in the mountains in six western states. Bryce Canyon in southern Utah is one of those places. Bristlecones are the world's oldest trees. Some, such as those growing in the White Mountains of California, are almost 5,000 years old! The bristlecone pines in Bryce Canyon are as old as 1,500 years.

After walking along for nearly a mile, they reached the turnoff to the Navajo Loop Trail. They took the second trail toward Wall Street.

The family entered a narrow canyon with towering red walls.

"I'll bet this is Wall Street," James said.

"So this is where I've lost all that money these last few years," Dad joked.

Mom laughed. "I think that one went right over their heads, but look at that Douglas fir growing way up toward the light. It's amazing what living things do to survive."

The family walked farther up the trail.

"Oh!" a woman shrieked.

Up ahead the woman collapsed on the ground. She crawled to a nearby log. "Ahh!" she moaned. The woman grabbed her ankle. Then she put her hand on her head and lay back on the log.

Morgan got to the woman first. "Are you okay?" she asked.

The woman looked up. "I hurt my ankle."

"Do you want us to take your shoes off?" Dad asked.

The woman put her hand over her eyes and thought for a moment. "Yes. That's probably a good idea. It's the left foot."

Mom gently untied the woman's shoelaces.

"Please stop," the woman called out. "My foot hurts too much."

"I can already see swelling above your ankle," Mom said.

"I flipped my foot over on the embankment," the woman said. "I stepped on some loose rock. My foot totally gave out."

Morgan pulled her sweatshirt from her pack and held it out. "Do you want this for a pillow?"

The woman looked up at Morgan. "That's awfully nice of you. This is what I get for hiking alone: the chance to get rescued by strangers."

"We're very nice," Morgan said. She slipped her sweatshirt under the woman's head and neck.

"Can you do me a favor and grab my water bottle?" the woman asked. "I'm very thirsty."

"Here you go," James said.

"Do you think you'll be able to hike out of here?" Morgan asked.

The woman slowly moved her foot. "Ah!" she called out. "I doubt it. I was having enough trouble hiking at this altitude without a bad ankle."

"We're going to have to get help," Dad said.

"I'll go to the rim and get a ranger," volunteered James.

"I'll go with him," Morgan added.

"Why don't I go with James," Mom said. "Morgan, you stay here with Dad and help out."

James and Mom took off up the trail.

"By the way," Morgan asked, "what's your name?"

"Colleen," the woman replied. "Believe it or not, I was a ranger here years ago. I used to hike these trails every day. This is my first time back."

"My mom and dad used to work at Zion years ago," Morgan said. "They're just coming back to southern Utah for the first time too."

A rainbow over Bryce Canyon

"Is that so?" Colleen asked, squinting and looking up. "I appreciate you keeping me company," she said, slowly sitting up. Colleen tried to turn her foot. "Oooh," she moaned, lying back down. "I guess I won't be doing that for a while."

"Is there anything we can do for you?" Morgan asked.

"How about getting my handkerchief wet and putting it on my forehead?" Colleen said.

Morgan found Colleen's handkerchief and dampened it. "Here you go," she said.

"Anything else?" Dad asked.

"Yes. I have some ibuprofen in the side pocket of my pack," Colleen said. "I think I could use a couple."

Morgan searched through Colleen's pack. She found the ibuprofen and held out two for Colleen.

"Could you keep talking to me?" Colleen asked. "It takes my mind off the pain."

"You said you were a ranger here years ago," Dad said. "What did you do?"

Colleen lay back down and closed her eyes. "Lots of things. Like lead hikes on this trail." She laughed. "I gave campfire talks, and I used to teach classes in the Junior Ranger Program." Colleen stopped talking and looked at Morgan. "For people your age."

OFFICIAL PATCH

Like many national parks, Bryce Canyon National Park has a Junior Ranger Program for children. This program gives kids a chance to learn about park history, wildlife, and geology. By participating in activities and learning about the park, Junior Rangers can receive official badges and patches.

"Until my husband died seven years ago, we spent a good part of every summer in a national park," Colleen said. She sighed and took a deep breath.

"You're lucky you got to work here," Morgan said. "I think I'm going to do the same thing when I grow up."

"Good for you," Colleen said. "By the way, what are your names?"

"I'm Morgan. This is my dad, Robert."

"Nice to meet both of you," Colleen said. "Although I wish we'd met under different circumstances." She looked around at the rocks. "Here we are stranded in Wall Street. Well, I guess there are worse places to be stuck."

Morgan and Dad laughed.

"You know what the Native American legend says about the rocks out here?" Colleen said.

"What?" Morgan asked.

"The Paiute Indians who lived around this area said a coyote turned the Legend People to stone. These people were really animals, but they had the power to look like people. Coyote built a village for these people to shelter them from the hot sun and desert winds. But once they had homes, the people defied Coyote. They didn't listen to him when he spoke. They said they no longer needed him. Coyote eventually became angry at the people and turned them into stone. Those people are the hoodoos we see now. I'm afraid I might have become a hoodoo myself if you hadn't come along."

"Excuse us! Look out!" A team of six rescuers hurried down the switchbacks, pushing a large one-wheeled wheelbarrow with a basket in the middle of it. Mom and James followed.

"Help is on the way!" Morgan announced.

"I can hear them," Colleen replied.

The rescue team arrived. Immediately, the rangers started treating Colleen. They checked her pulse and blood pressure. They asked her questions. They put an air splint on her ankle to keep it from moving. Then they radioed for an ambulance.

The rescuers hoisted Colleen onto the wheeled litter and strapped her down.

"Thanks for your help," Colleen called out to the family as she was wheeled away.

A ranger stayed behind to talk with the family for a moment. "It looks like she may have broken her ankle," she said. "Unfortunately, it's a common injury out here."

"Where are they taking her?" Morgan asked.

"Probably to a hospital in Panguitch," the ranger answered. "But I've got to go and catch up with them." The ranger trotted up the trail.

"I hope Colleen's going to be okay," Morgan said.

"Come on," Mom said. "Let's get through Wall Street and up to the rim."

"And watch our steps along the way," James said.

The family hiked up the rest of the Navajo Loop Trail.

Another pretty view of the canyon

James ran up to his parents. "Guess what I just saw?"

"What?" Mom asked.

"Four of Jupiter's moons!" James replied.

"Really?" Dad asked.

"Maybe we should have waited in your line," Mom said.

"No wonder the night sky program is so popular here," Dad said. He looked at the long lines of people at the telescopes.

"The ranger said the high elevation lets us see into space better," James said.

"And there are no city lights around," Morgan added. "That makes the stars appear brighter."

A ranger walked by.

"Hi," Morgan said, "remember us?"

The ranger looked at Morgan for a second but didn't say anything.

"We were there when you helped rescue that woman today," Morgan explained.

"That's right," the ranger answered. "She might have been stuck there for quite a while if you weren't around to help her. We just found out that Colleen broke her ankle. She's spending the night at the hospital in Panguitch. She told me on the way up that she couldn't wait to come back and finish hiking."

"As soon as she gets her cast off, maybe she can," James said.

"I bet she's going to try," the ranger said.

The ranger looked around at all the people. "These telescopes are really a treat, aren't they?" she said. "People come to Bryce to see the canyon. But they also get to view the night sky."

"I got to see the rings around Saturn," Morgan said. "It was pretty cool!"

"I think I'll take a peek in a telescope myself," the ranger said, heading over to one.

Back at camp, James lay in his sleeping bag and stared up through the mesh of his tent. He tried to pick out the constellations that the ranger had talked about. He could make out the Big Dipper, and Hercules, and …

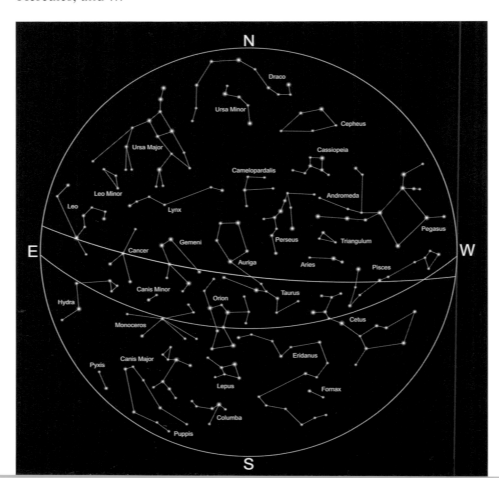

James rolled over, flicked on his flashlight, and wrote in his journal.

Tuesday, July 18, 10:30 p.m.

Dear Diary,

This is James Parker reporting again. I'm going to see if we can get a telescope for back home. Seeing the stars and planets is amazing. And the rock formations here are neat too. They're all so different. I want to explore more at Bryce. Maybe next time we can backpack overnight along the Under-the-Rim Trail. That would be cool. But Mom and Dad say our hikes in Zion are going to be longer, so we have to leave Bryce tomorrow. I'll miss you, Bryce. But I will be back!

Sincerely,

James

Morgan was curled on her side, already asleep in her tent. Her diary was left wide open on her sleeping bag. She'd written:

Tuesday, July 18, 10:00 p.m.

Dear Diary,

What a great day we had in my first national park! We hiked on the Peekaboo Trail yesterday and the Queen's Garden and Navajo Trails today. James and I pretended we were servants of the queen. How fun.

Mom and Dad said if we pack up early tomorrow morning, we'll have enough time to drive the whole park road to Rainbow Point. Mom says there are even older bristlecone pines out there. I'd like to see them.

We saw this woman, Colleen, get hurt on the trail today. Then she got rescued. I hope she's going to be okay. I wish we could stay in touch. I hope I go hiking here when I'm her age.

Well, I'm really tired. More soon.

Good night,

Morgan

It looks like a chess game, doesn't it?

The next morning, the family packed up their campsite and drove to Rainbow and Yovimpa Points. They stopped to see some of the great views along the way, and they hiked the Bristlecone Loop Trail at Rainbow Point.

"Maybe next time we can take some of the other trails," Dad said.

"But for now we'd better get going," Mom added.

But Morgan and James did talk their parents into one more thing.

"We can park our car at Sunset Point," James said, "and then take the bus over to Bryce Point and hike back."

"It will be an easy walk," Morgan added. "And, besides, when's the next time we'll be here again, anyway?"

"I'm glad to see you like it here," Mom said.

"I think they've convinced us," Dad said. "So we'll get to Zion a little later."

"Here we are at Bryce Point!" Morgan announced. She

stood up and hopped off the bus. Her family followed. They started hiking the rim trail.

"We're walking right on the edge of the canyon," James said. "Look at the views!"

"It sounds like you two are our tour guides," Mom said, smiling.

"Can you think of any better guides?" James asked.

Morgan pulled out her camera. "I want to get lots of pictures before we go."

"I think these are the best views of the canyon we've seen so far," Dad said. "I can see why you want to take pictures."

The family continued walking along the rim.

"Hey, look!" James called out. "You can see the trail we were on yesterday. It's right down there." He pointed into the canyon.

Down below the family saw the winding path of the Navajo Trail heading toward Wall Street.

"This is quite a view," Mom said. "And it's so peaceful. In this part of the park, it's like we have the whole place to ourselves."

"It looks to me like a huge chess game," James said. "Look, there are the two castles surrounding the board." He pointed to two pillars in the canyon that were taller than the rest.

"Checkmate," Morgan declared.

"Uh-uh," James retorted.

"Remember, my queen is way over there." He pointed to the Queen's Garden area.

The family hiked on. When they arrived at Sunset Point overlook, they saw crowds of people gathered there.

"I guess this is where all the people are," Mom announced.

"With a view like this, no wonder," Dad said.

Morgan asked one of the tourists if he would take a picture of her family.

The family gathered at the edge of the railing, put their arms around each other, and smiled.

"Ready?" the tourist asked.

"Ready!" the family said, smiling.

He took the picture.

"Well, it's time for one last look, and then we have to say good-bye," Dad announced.

"For now," James said. "I don't know about you guys, but Morgan and I are coming back!"

After looking into Bryce Canyon one more time, the family turned and walked back to the parking lot. They got into their car and drove out of the park.

While Dad drove, Mom pulled out her journal and wrote:

Wednesday, July 19, 12:00 noon

Dear Diary,

I can't believe it has taken so long for Robert and me to come back to Bryce. Morgan and James loved it too. I think they want to work here when they're older. I'm all for that! It will give Robert and me a great excuse to come visit.

Bryce is so interesting. I really want to learn more about the bristlecone pines. And I hear condors have returned to the area. That's exciting, because they were nearly extinct a few years ago.

But the best thing about Bryce is the canyon itself. We all enjoyed coming up with names for the rock formations. I think the "Alien" was best. And could there be anything more beautiful than Bryce Canyon on the planet?

I guess we'll find out when we get to Zion!

Sincerely,

Kristen

"We're coming to the turnoff to Zion," Dad announced. "I'm going to pull over here for gas."

"It's only a few more miles to the park," James said, looking at the map.

Morgan looked over James's shoulder. "It's so close to Bryce. We've hardly driven at all."

"And to the Grand Canyon," Dad said. "That's why this whole area is called the Grand Circle. There is so much to see within a small area."

After stopping, the family piled back into the car. Mom took over driving. They headed toward Zion National Park's east entrance.

"We may be close to Bryce," Dad said, "but the scenery is a world apart. You'll see."

While Mom drove, Dad pulled out his journal.

Wednesday, July 19, 3:00 p.m.
Dear Diary,
Well, after all these years, I'm happy to say that Bryce is in great shape. I'm so glad that America has national parks that protect and preserve our most beautiful lands. And Bryce certainly is one of them. The rock formations and colors of the rock are incredible. We hiked a bunch of trails too. I'm glad Morgan and James like to hike! And they're better at it than I am.
Anyway, here we are, heading toward Zion—

James tapped Dad on the shoulder. "Dad, look up!"
Dad quickly wrote in his journal,

Oops. Gotta go!
More later.
Robert

"We're coming to the park!" James said.

Mom stopped at the park entrance station. She showed the ranger their annual park pass and was given a map and newspaper. They drove into the park.

CONSERVE, ENJOY

National Park Mission Statement: National Parks were created to "conserve the scenery and the natural and historic objects and the wildlife therein and to provide for the enjoyment of the same in such manner and by such means as will leave them unimpaired for the enjoyment of future generations."—National Park Service

"Look at this place!" Morgan called out.

"Look at the color of the road!" Mom said. "It's the same color as the cliffs."

Mom slowed the car down. The family stared out the windows at the massive orange and red cliffs, buttes, mesas, and gullies.

"This place is amazing!" James said.

"It sure is," Mom agreed. "There's a turnout up ahead. I'm going to pull over."

"I remember this," Dad said, "the Checkerboard Mesa."

Mom stopped the car, and the family got out. In front of them was a large flat-topped pyramid-shaped mountain. There were vertical and horizontal lines etched across the mesa's cliff face.

"This is surreal," Dad said. "And look, there are mountains like this all over the place."

Morgan got out her camera and took several photos.

FUTURISTIC SHAPES

In the eastern part of Zion, there are many fascinating patterns of erosion on the cliffs and rocks. Perhaps the best known is on Checkerboard Mesa. Its orange and red sandstone face has fantastic vertical and horizontal shapes. The horizontal lines are from layers of sand that were deposited by the wind during ancient times. Repeated freezing created vertical grooves or cracks. Checkerboard Mesa faces north, where it takes longer for ice to melt. This gives the ice more time to help create these spectacular patterns in the rocks.

We don't see rocks like these back hom'

"I've never seen anything like this!" Mom gasped.

"That's what you said at Bryce," James reminded her.

"That's true," Mom said. "But I've never seen anything like Bryce either."

"But Mom, you worked here before," Morgan remembered.

"That's true too," Mom said. "I guess I forgot how amazing this is."

"Wait till you see the rest of the park," Dad said to everyone.

The family got back in the car. They drove by more bizarre rock formations in the eastern part of Zion.

After a few miles, they came to a line of cars. Mom pulled up behind them.

"I wonder what happened," Morgan said.

"They're just making cars wait to go through the tunnel," Dad said.

"When there are campers and RVs in there, there's only room for one-way traffic."

"Hey, I've got an idea," Morgan said. "Instead of waiting here in line, why don't we do the Canyon Overlook hike? It starts right there." She pointed to a trail sign.

"You really did your research," Dad said.

Morgan held up the park newspaper. "The hike's listed in here."

"Well?" Mom asked.

"Sure," Dad answered.

Mom pulled over and parked the car.

The family hiked a winding trail with catwalks and steep overlooks. After a half mile, they came to a metal railing overlooking Zion Canyon.

They stood at the edge. Below them was the park road, which zigzagged down to the bottom of the canyon. The family stood and enjoyed the view.

Our first look at Zion Canyon

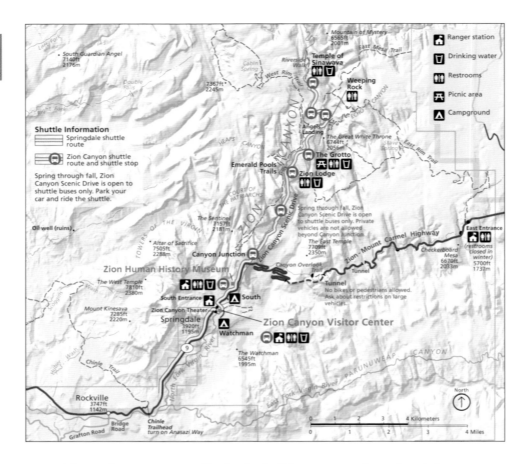

Shuttle Information

Springdale shuttle route

Zion Canyon shuttle route and shuttle stop

Spring through fall, Zion Canyon Scenic Drive is open to shuttle buses only. Park your car and ride the shuttle.

Ranger station
Drinking water
Restrooms
Picnic area
Campground

After a few moments, Dad asked, "Are you ready to head down into Zion Canyon?"

"Yes," Morgan, James, and Mom answered.

The family hiked back to their car. They waited in line for a few minutes and then followed the cars through the tunnel.

"It's long!" James said.

"Very," Dad replied. "It was the longest tunnel through sandstone in the United States when it was first built."

Soon they were out of the tunnel. Mom turned off the headlights. The road wove its way down into the desert heat of Zion Canyon.

"A drop of water just hit me," James called out. "Me too," Morgan said.

"And another. And another," James said.

Morgan and James stood under Zion Canyon's Weeping Rock.

LONG JOURNEY

Geologists estimate that the rainwater from the east side of the canyon that percolates through to such places as Weeping Rock takes as long as 1,000 to 4,000 years to get from the top of the mountain to the hanging gardens below. The water percolates out at springs and hanging gardens. It takes so long for water to arrive at the springs because there is 2,000 feet of Navajo Sandstone to pass through.

"It's pretty hot here, isn't it?" Dad asked James and Morgan.

"It's a lot hotter than Bryce," Morgan replied. "This feels good," she said as more drops plunked down on her head.

MINUS 4,000 FEET

Although Zion and Bryce are relatively close together, the weather at each park is very different. This is mostly due to elevation. Zion Canyon's elevation is around 4,000 feet. Most of Bryce is near 8,000 feet, making Bryce cooler. Average summer temperatures at Bryce are pleasant, with temperatures reaching highs of seventy to eighty degrees and lows in the forties. At Zion, the average summer temperature is more than ninety degrees, and it often rises above one hundred. Nighttime lows in the summer are in the sixties.

I think these hanging gardens are beautiful," Mom said. She looked at all the green moss and ferns underneath Weeping Rock. "You don't expect to see this in the desert."

"This area reminds me of Menu Falls, the waterfall we saw on the bus tour," James said.

"I like the fact that Zion's buses have viewing windows," Dad said. "And Mom and I can enjoy all the scenery with you."

Weeping Rock, nice and cool

Zion National Park offers a free shuttle service for park visitors. The shuttle service takes people to most park locations and runs as often as every six minutes. Before the shuttle service, many of Zion's most popular places were packed with cars. Up to 5,000 cars competed for only 400 to 500 parking spaces in Zion Canyon each day. Now, cars aren't allowed at all in upper Zion Canyon.

"Yeah, some of the tallest cliffs in the world are here," Morgan said. "And we're going to be on top of one tomorrow: Angels Landing."

"I'm getting cold," James said, jumping out of the way of the dripping water.

"What do you guys want to do next?" Morgan asked.

"We could take the bus to the lodge," James suggested, "then do the Emerald Pools hike."

"We did want to go there," Mom said.

"And it's only a short hike," Dad added.

"And when we finish, we're back at the lodge," Morgan said.

"From what I remember, Emerald Pools is one of the most beautiful places in the park," Dad said.

"I think we're going hiking," Mom laughed.

The family walked down from Weeping Rock to the bus stop. They got on the shuttle heading to Zion Lodge and the Emerald Pools trailhead.

The family crossed the footbridge over the Virgin River. They took the Lower Emerald Pools Trail.

"The clouds are building up again," Dad observed, looking up at the sky.

"A thunderstorm would be great today," James said. "At least it would cool us off."

"Yeah, and we wouldn't have to hike up the canyon to get out of the rain like we did at Bryce," Morgan added.

"Still, we better watch the sky," Mom warned. "Those clouds are really brewing."

After hiking a short distance, the family came to a large rock alcove. Above it were two waterfalls. The trail followed a railing behind the waterfalls.

"It looks kind of like the Weeping Rock area," Morgan said.

"Only bigger," Dad added.

"And it has more of these hanging gardens," Mom noticed. "It's so green in here."

Around Emerald
Pools—one of our
favorite places in
the park

"It's like a little oasis in the desert," James said. "It's so much wetter than the other parts of the park."

James stuck out his hand and moved it back and forth trying to touch the gentle spray of one of the waterfalls. "Hey! It's blowing in the wind."

"Maybe it just doesn't want you to touch it." Morgan laughed.

The family hiked around the waterfalls to a small connecting trail that led to the middle pool.

"Shall we?" Mom asked.

They all looked up at the billowing clouds.

"I don't know how much longer we have," Dad said.

"Please? It's only a short trail," Morgan pleaded.

"You talked us into it again," Dad said. "Maybe the rain will wait."

They climbed a series of rocky switchbacks. Soon they were at a small pool above the waterfall.

"I wonder what animals come to drink here?" James said.

RINGTAIL CAT

Zion is home to many types of animals. The most commonly seen mammals include mule deer, gray foxes, ringtail, striped skunk, desert cottontail, and black-tailed jackrabbit. Mountain lions live at Zion but are rarely seen.

"Just lions, and tigers, and bears," Morgan joked.

"Yeah, right," James said.

Dad looked at the connector trail to the Upper Emerald Pool.

"We've come this far," he said. "We may as well go all the way to the top."

"It's only three-tenths of a mile," James said.

After climbing up the rocky, sandy trail, the family came to a large pool at the base of gigantic red cliffs. It was cool and shady at the pool, which was surrounded by trees and giant boulders.

"Now this looks like a Shangri-la!" Mom exclaimed.

"Unbelievable," Dad said. "It's gorgeous up here."

The family put their packs down and began exploring the sandy area near the pools.

"We used to be able to swim up here," Dad said, "back when I worked at Zion."

"They don't allow that anymore because swimming stirs up the algae, and that ruins the pool," Mom explained.

"I'm sure people prefer it to be peaceful up here anyway," Dad said, "instead of having a bunch of swimmers."

"Hey, look at these!" James exclaimed. He pointed to hundreds of pollywogs in the water.

"Canyon treefrogs," Mom observed. "That's what they'll become."

Zion Canyon treefrogs are highly unusual. They're 1¼ to 2¼ inches long; typically brown, gray, or olive in color; and have faint dark patches on their backs. These frogs have an unusual mating call that sounds like a sheep bleating. Visitors to Zion sometimes mistake the sound for sheep.

Dad looked up at the cliffs. "Hello up there!" he called out.

"Hellooo … up … there!" the cliffs echoed.

"Hey!" James shouted.

"Hey! … Hey! … Hey!" the cliffs replied.

"Hey," Morgan whispered, "I think it's starting to rain. Look at the drops in the pool."

"You're right," Mom said.

The rain started coming down harder. The family moved under a tree.

James gazed up at the gray clouds. "Look how dark the sky is," he observed.

"I just saw lightning," Morgan called out.

A distant rumble echoed throughout the canyon. The rain started coming down harder. Upper Emerald Pool was showered with raindrops.

"I think it's too late to make a run for it," Dad said.

"This ought to teach us a lesson," Mom said. "When you're hiking, you should be prepared for all kinds of weather."

"Good thing I brought these," Dad said. He pulled out some beach towels. "I thought we might sit by the river after our hike."

Dad draped the two towels over his family. They huddled close together, watching the rain hitting the pool. Lightning flashed. Thunder rumbled in the distance. The rain soaked the towels.

"The weather sure changes quickly out here," Dad said.

MONSOONS

Each summer tropical moisture flows up from the Gulf of Mexico toward the southwestern United States. This typically happens from around July 15 until September 15. This period of time is called the monsoon season. The result is that Zion and Bryce often get afternoon thunderstorms at this time of the year.

"I know, I'm cold!" James said. The family huddled closer. Dad put his arms around his twins. "Body warmth: It's the best remedy for the cold."

The rain poured down and showered off the rocks near Emerald Pool.

Lightning flashed again. Thunder rumbled loudly.

"It's a good thing we're not at the top of the rim this time," James said.

"And a good thing we're not in the Narrows today!" Dad exclaimed.

After a few minutes, James stepped out from under the trees. "I think it's letting up." He heard the sound of water thundering down and turned around.

"You guys have to see this!" James said.

Morgan, Mom, and Dad joined James.

Tumbling off the cliff behind Emerald Pool was a brand-new, mud-colored waterfall.

"I don't remember ever seeing waterfalls like this here," Mom said. "Boy, we are lucky!"

"It looks like we're in Yosemite," Dad observed.

The rain dwindled to a gentle mist.

"This really does look like a Shangri-la," Morgan said.

"And we're the lucky ones out here who get to see it," Dad said.

Something dark flitted about in the air. James watched its silhouette against the darkening sky.

"There's another over here!" Morgan called out. "And another!"

"The bats are coming out," Mom said. "It's getting dark."

"We better get going before there's no light left," Dad warned. He flicked on his penlight. "Follow me."

The family wrung out the towels and hiked back down the Upper Pool Trail. Soon they came to Middle Emerald Pool. The waterfall there was also pouring over the cliff. They looked back and saw the huge new waterfall above the Upper Pool.

"This is a once-in-a-lifetime experience," Dad said.

"That's true," Mom said, "but I sure hope our tents are dry."

"Yeah, we forgot about that," James said. "It's a good thing we put our rain flies up before we left."

The family hiked back in the twilight. Bats flitted about in search of bugs. Toads that had emerged during the rain hopped out of the way as the family approached.

"We better watch our step," Dad warned.

They reached a bend in the trail. Dad stopped and took another look back at the falls, which were still visible in the night sky. "I just don't want to forget this," he said. "How many people get to see a roaring waterfall like this at Zion?"

Then they turned and walked back to the lodge.

"Okay, are you ready?" Morgan asked her parents. "Ready," Mom and Dad said while holding each other.

"When I say three, *kiss!*" Morgan looked through the camera lens. She adjusted the zoom. "One. Two. Three." Her parents looked at each other and then kissed. Morgan snapped the picture.

"It's too bad we didn't have romantic music playing in the background," James joked.

"What do you mean?" Dad said. "I thought we did!"

"That was perfect," Morgan said. "I got you two smooching and all of Zion Canyon in the background."

The trail to Angels Landing

We went out there?!

"That *was* perfect," Mom agreed. "Just as it was when your father and I first met here twenty years ago."

"You really met right here?" James asked.

"Right here, on this very trail," Dad said. "We both hiked up here on our day off."

"I was working at the park visitor center," Mom said. "I think I had seen your dad there a few times, but we never spoke."

"I was working at the lodge," Dad said. "When I saw your mom up here, I knew it was my lucky day."

"Kind of like destiny," Morgan said.

"That's right, destiny," Mom agreed. "Come here, you two." She hugged her twins as they all stood together on the top of Angels Landing.

"It's amazing up here, isn't it?" Morgan asked, looking down at the canyon below.

"There's a bus on the road!" James called out. "It looks so tiny."

"Don't get too close to that cliff," Mom warned, reaching for James's arm.

"I'm all right," James said.

"It's only a 1,500-foot drop," Dad said. "Straight down. You can understand our worry."

The family looked around at the view. From the top of Angels Landing, they could see all of Zion Canyon, including the Weeping Rock Trail. Across the canyon were the Great White Throne and Cable Mountain. Farther up the canyon, the cliffs got closer together, and the road disappeared at the Temple of Sinawava.

"That's where we're going to be tomorrow?" Morgan asked, looking toward the end of the road.

"Actually, the day after," Dad said. "It will take us two days to get there and then out of the Narrows."

"We would have been going there today," Mom said, "but the

rangers recommended against it. There's still a chance of thunderstorms this afternoon, believe it or not." Mom looked up at the clear skies. "So there's a chance of high water. It's too dangerous to be in there today."

FLASH FLOODS

Hiking in Zion's canyons can be dangerous. Flash floods do happen, and in many cases, there is no escape because the trail is surrounded by high cliffs. Safety depends on hikers using sound judgment, being prepared, and paying attention, including to the latest weather reports. Weather reports at Zion include the potential for flash floods.

"I can understand that," James said, "after all the water we saw pouring off the cliffs yesterday."

"Yeah. We wouldn't want to be caught in the Narrows during a storm like that," Dad said. "But the weather's supposed to be much better tomorrow."

"Besides," Mom added, "we can head back to camp early today and get our gear ready to go. We're getting up early tomorrow for the shuttle ride. It's going to be a long day."

The family looked out over Zion Canyon and enjoyed the view. Other hikers came up, and Morgan asked one of them to take the family's picture. They ate some snacks and then headed back down the chains and rails on the steep Angels Landing Trail.

RAILS & CHAINS

WARNING! Do not attempt to hike up Angels Landing if you are afraid of heights! This popular trail in Zion is five miles round-trip and climbs 1,488 feet. The last half mile follows a very narrow trail up a ridge. Chains have been added to make it safer. But there are long drop-offs and slippery footing in this part of the trail. Be careful!

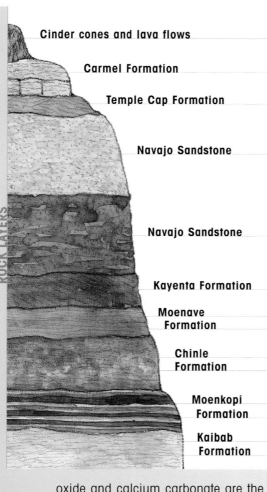

Cinder cones and lava flows

Carmel Formation

Temple Cap Formation

Navajo Sandstone

Navajo Sandstone

Kayenta Formation

Moenave Formation

Chinle Formation

Moenkopi Formation

Kaibab Formation

There are four steps to Zion's geology:

1. **Sedimentation.** The area that makes up Zion was once part of the world's largest desert. Layers of rock and soil started building up millions of years ago. Navajo sandstone makes up the big cliffs of Zion. Zion's sandstone cliffs are 2,000 to 3,000 feet high, making them some of the steepest cliffs in the world.

2. **Lithification.** The weight of the sediment pushing downward turned the sand into stone. Minerals helped cement the rocks. Iron oxide and calcium carbonate are the key minerals holding the sandstone together. Iron oxide is a rust color, creating the red rocks. Calcium carbonate is white and is seen on some of Zion's cliffs.

3. **Uplift.** The drifting continental plates that make up Earth's crust collided, causing uplift of the rocks and cliffs that make up the area around Zion. About 10,000 feet of uplift has occurred at Zion and is still going on today.

4. **Erosion.** Zion Canyon was cut by the Virgin River. Most of this cutting was due to "thousand-year floods." These floods will occur again sometime in the future.

"That was some hike," Mom said after the family crossed the foot-bridge at the Grotto parking lot.

James looked up to the top of Angels Landing. "I can't believe we hiked all the way up there."

"But you did!" Dad exclaimed. "And I'm proud of both of you."

"I think we're ready for the Narrows," Morgan said. "I can't wait."

"You know," Mom said, looking at the river, "we do have a few hours before we have to go to the visitor center to get our permit. Why don't we find a nice shady area by the river and ... "

"Swim," James said.

"I'm all for that!" Morgan exclaimed.

That's where the family spent the rest of the afternoon, keeping cool in the water of the river and reading in the shade.

The family hopped off the van. "Well, this is it," James said. He grabbed his walking stick and then hoisted his backpack onto his back. "Ugh, this weighs a lot!"

"Good-bye, civilization," Morgan said.

"And hello, Narrows!" Dad added.

"You sure you have everything?" the driver of the van asked. "We've got extra water in the back if you need to fill up."

"I think we're okay," Dad answered. "And we've got a water filter with us, anyway. But thanks."

"You're never far from water on this trail," the driver said. "And the Narrows has some of the most amazing scenery in the world. Good luck, and be careful." The driver turned the van around and headed back up the dirt road.

"I guess this really is it," Mom said.

"To the Narrows we go!" Morgan proclaimed. "Come on." She led the way along a dirt road. The road passed a ranch that was on a plateau high above the canyons of Zion. Pinyon pines, ponderosas, and junipers dotted the hills. A tiny stream paralleled the road.

"I can't believe that's the river," James said, "it seems so small."

"Just wait," Dad said.

The family walked quietly along the road. They passed an old, abandoned cabin. The only sounds they heard were birds chirping overhead, the gurgling water, and their shuffling feet.

"There's nobody up here," Dad said.

"That means we'll get the Narrows all to ourselves," James replied.

After about an hour, the trail dipped down.

"Here we go!" Morgan exclaimed, walking toward the river.

The family crisscrossed the river. It was about ten feet wide and a few inches deep. Soon they entered a gorge colored cliffs.

"Now this looks more like Zion!" Dad said.

The family walked farther into the Virgin River Narrows. They tromped back and forth from one side of the river to the other. Each time they left the river, they tried to follow faint paths created by hikers who came before them. The trail on each side was full of rocks and boulders. Some were wet and slippery. They used their walking sticks to help keep their balance, especially while carrying their heavy packs.

Morgan walked ahead.

The canyon walls got narrower and steeper. At times, it was as if they were entering a crack in the ground and hiking into the under-world—a dark, forbidding place where no one goes. Morgan kept snapping pictures.

The farther they walked, the cooler and shadier it got. In some places, the sun's rays hardly made it through the slit between the two canyon walls rising high above them. In other places, the canyon opened up and plants and trees grew alongside the river. Sometimes the trail left the river, and for a short time, the family could hike on dry ground. Then they would turn another bend and enter into a narrower, darker gorge.

Morgan took another picture.

"You're going to use up your battery," James said, catching up to her.

"I've got extras," Morgan said. "And, besides, when are we ever going to be in here again?"

"Good point," Dad said.

They hiked on. The sound of the river and the rhythm of their walking seemed to put the family into a trance. One step, then another. Then the walking stick. Then another step.

At times, the trail passed through deeper water. And for short periods, the family waded through small pools several feet deep. After each pool, they stepped over rocks to shallower water at the side of the river before hiking back into a deeper part of the stream.

They passed a yellow post.

"I wonder what that's for?" Morgan said.

James pulled out his map. "I think we just entered the national park. Look, I think we're right here." He pointed to the map, just past the first narrows.

"That means we've hiked over three and a half hours!" James said.

"It sure went quickly," Dad said. "That's why I put my watch in my pack, so I don't worry about time."

"The first campsite isn't far away," James said. He folded up his map, put it in his pocket, and walked on.

A few feet later, he stopped.

A large dead bird was on the trail. Its feathers were torn up and strewn about. It looked like part of its body had been eaten.

"It looks like a hawk," Mom said.

Morgan stepped around the bird and continued on the trail. The rest of the family followed. They turned a bend and came to a side canyon.

"Let's go check it out," James said.

The family put their packs down and headed up the narrow gorge that followed a dry streambed. The polished rocks of the tiny canyon were orange colored.

Deep, dark, and narrow

"I've seen pictures of these small canyons before," Dad said. "But it's much better actually being in one."

The side canyon quickly dead-ended. Morgan took a few more pictures. Then they walked back to their packs and continued hiking along the main trail through the river.

The farther they hiked, the higher the canyon walls became.

"Now we're getting into some serious Narrows!" James exclaimed.

"You said that a few minutes ago," Morgan reminded him.

"It was true too, a few minutes ago," Mom said.

They walked past an arch cut high in the canyon wall. It was full of streaks where rain poured down during storms.

"I'll bet there was a big waterfall there the other day," Morgan said.

They hiked on, splashing through the river and attempting to follow any trail.

"Now this is a real adventure," Mom said.

"I think I'm getting hypnotized by the sound of the water," Dad said. "I feel like I'm in a lost world without any concept of time."

"Look, swiss cheese rocks!" James called out. He pointed to dozens of small holes in a rock wall.

Morgan walked toward a shallow area upstream. A trail led out of the water. She made her way toward it. The family followed her. They walked over sand and mud and around rocks. The trail continued over a small hill and around some trees and shrubs.

"We might as well keep dry as long as we can," Morgan said.

"Yeah, but look at my shoes," James said. "They're full of mud."

"We'll sure need a good wash when we get back, clothes and all," Dad said.

Morgan froze.

A sandy-gray snake with fierce eyes was coiled five feet in front of her. The tip of its beaded tail stood upright, rattling back and forth. Its dark tongue poked in and out of its mouth.

Morgan stared at the snake.

The snake stared back.

James bumped into Morgan's back, pushing her forward.

"A rattlesnake!" Morgan screamed, leaping to the side.

The snake pulled into a tighter curl and rattled its tail again.

James grabbed Morgan's arm and pulled her back.

"It's a rattler!" James said to his parents as they walked up. "What do we do now?" Morgan asked. "It's right on the trail."

"Give it a few moments," Mom said, moving to the front.

Mom slowly held out her walking stick in the direction of the rattler.

The rattler wound up tightly, pulled its head back in a striking pose, and then rattled its tail again.

"I guess that wasn't such a good idea," Mom said. She pulled her stick away and backed the family up a few more feet.

"We can always hike through the river," James suggested. "It's not like we don't already have our feet wet."

"True," Mom said, "but the water looks treacherous right here."

"I don't think we'll have to," Morgan said. "Look."

The rattler slowly slithered toward the bushes above the trail. It kept its eyes on the family as it moved sideways to a shady spot then stopped.

"A lot of good that will do us," Dad said.

"It's only a few feet from the trail," Morgan observed.

The rattler lay in the shade, flicking its tongue in and out.

Mom took a step forward. "It's still too close," she said. "Go on, rattler. Head up the hill. Go on."

But the snake didn't move.

"How about this," James suggested, "we can walk close to the edge of the water on those rocks. That will get us away from the snake."

Mom followed James's cue. She stepped down onto a rock and balanced herself. "This will work," she said. "I'll stay here and give everyone a hand."

BEING BITTEN IS A SERIOUS PROBLEM

There are more than 8,000 venomous snakebites in the United States each year, but fewer than ten deaths. Venomous snakes, such as rattlers, can cause severe pain and long-lasting tissue damage.

Being bitten by a snake is a serious problem, but it doesn't have to be fatal. The following are suggestions for treating a snakebite:

1. Get away from the snake. Call 911 as soon as possible, if you can.
2. Keep the victim calm and still. The less the victim moves, the less the venom spreads.
3. Have the victim lie down with the affected limb lower than the heart. Keep the limb still.
4. Treat the victim for shock and keep him or her warm.
5. Remove any rings, bracelets, boots, or restricting items. The bitten area will swell.
6. Apply two lightly constricting bands two inches above and below the bite. Use soft material such as a handkerchief. Make the band as tight as a nurse does when giving a blood pressure test. Do not make the bands too tight.
7. Wash the bite with soap and water, if available.
8. If the victim has to walk out, let him or her sit for twenty to thirty minutes. This helps prevent the venom from spreading.
9. Get medical care for the victim.
10. DO NOT cut the victim's skin at the bite, put your mouth on the bite and suck out the venom, or apply a tourniquet.

One by one, the family stepped onto the rocks. Mom gave everyone a hand as they went by. As they passed, they looked up at the snake to make sure it stayed a safe distance away. And then they hopped off the rocks and back up to the trail.

"Whew, that was close," Mom said.

"My heart was pounding," Morgan added.

"We're lucky," Mom said, stepping to the front of the group. "Getting bit by a rattler is something we definitely don't want to have happen, especially in here."

"It would have taken a long time to rescue me," Morgan said.

"I don't even want to think about it," Dad said.

Farther along, the trail disappeared back into the water. The river was twenty feet wide, and the canyon walls rose more than a thousand feet above them.

"I can hardly see the sky," James said.

"We're getting into the 'No Way Out' zone," Dad said. "If there was a flash flood, we'd be trapped."

The trail climbed out of the water again and up a small, sandy hill. It went through a crack between some rocks, then down a hill. At the bottom of the hill, the trail came back to the water.

"Look!" Morgan said, catching up to her father.

About twenty feet upstream was a small waterfall. It plunged into a deep pool of water.

"It's beautiful," Mom said.

"I know," Morgan replied, pulling out her camera. She started snapping pictures while Dad walked up the narrow streambed. James followed him.

But the water quickly went up to their waists.

Dad and James walked back to Morgan and took off their packs. Using their walking sticks as guides, they slowly navigated the river toward the waterfall.

"It's cold in here," James called out. "And my clothes are soaked!"

James stopped and watched his father take a few more steps. Dad was a few feet from the waterfall when he turned around. "The rocks are so polished in here."

Morgan snapped a few pictures of Dad and James near the waterfall. Then they clambered out.

The family found a rare sunny spot. They stretched out in the sun to warm up, dry out their clothes, and eat.

One of several waterfalls in the Narrows

The trail went into the shade once again as they hiked on into the deepening canyon.

"This is by far the narrowest spot we've come to," Dad said. He looked up at the canyon walls towering more than a thousand feet above them. He watched his family carefully navigate across the slippery rocks in the river.

"Now I know why they say it's like walking on bowling balls with moss on them," Morgan said.

"And all that with a pack on!" Mom added.

"Just take your time," Dad said. "Make sure each step is firm."

The family passed a signpost for the second campsite. They came upon Deep Creek junction. It was a wide stream with more water in it than the Virgin River.

They stopped to filter water from Deep Creek before trekking on.

They waded through the river, crisscrossing over rocks and small rapids. Occasionally, they found a dry spot to walk on. They passed several more campsites and came to Kolob Creek junction.

James pulled out his map. "We're getting close. We're only about fifty minutes from camp."

Morgan gazed at the dry creekbed of Kolob Creek.

Dad read his daughter's mind: "Do you want to check it out?"

Morgan nodded.

The four walked out of the river and toward Kolob Creek. They set their backpacks up against some rocks and trudged up the creek's canyon.

They walked until they saw a massive, partially formed arch. Red, brown, and black horizontal streaks on the canyon walls showed where past water levels had been. The floor of the canyon was full of maple trees.

"I wouldn't want to be in here during a flash flood," Morgan said. "It's as narrow as the Narrows."

"Look!" said Mom. "Deer tracks." She pointed to some fresh prints in the mud.

"I wonder how they got in here," James said.

The family hiked up a few more bends in the cool, dark side canyon. For a while, they followed the deer tracks embedded in the mud.

"Maybe we better head back," Mom suggested. "We still have a ways to go to our campsite."

"You're right," Dad said. "We don't want to be tramping through the river much longer today."

They turned around and headed back to their packs at the junction. They walked through the river and then up side trails, passing by several more campsites. Soon they came to spot number ten. It was a large, flat sandy area about ten feet from the river, with plenty of room to pitch their tents. Above it were some cliffs and overhanging rocks.

"I can't believe what an incredible campsite this is!" Dad exclaimed. He slowly peeled off his backpack.

"Well, there's no place like home," Morgan said.

"And what a home this is!" Mom added.

They took off their packs and set up camp.

In the morning, Mom got up first. Dawn was just breaking, but she got out of her tent and sat on a nearby rock to read. The Virgin River gurgled steadily along just a few feet away.

Morgan crawled out of her tent and yawned and stretched. "Hi, Mom!" she said.

"How'd you sleep?" Mom asked.

"Great," Morgan said. "I remember looking up at the stars through my tent. And the next thing I knew, it was morning."

"The sound of rushing water sure makes it easy to sleep out here," Mom said.

"Hey, you brought your book," Morgan commented. "Wasn't that too heavy to carry?"

"It was worth it. Reading is one of the things I like to do most while on vacation."

Morgan stood up and looked around. A few small trees and grasses lined the river. The steep canyon walls were orange, red, and dark gray. "We sure got a great campsite," Morgan said.

"I think all the spots we passed were great," Mom said. "But you're right. Ours may be the best. The sand here is soft under our tent, and we're right next to the river."

A few minutes later, Dad and James also awoke.

Mom and James cooked oatmeal for breakfast on the backpacking stove. Dad and Morgan sliced bananas and got out dried fruit and juice.

After breakfast, they packed up. While Mom and Dad folded up their tent, Morgan and James went over to the river to write in their journals.

Saturday, July 22

Dear Diary,

This is the first time I have ever backpacked overnight. But I know it won't be my last. We picked the perfect spot too. It's campsite #10 in the Narrows! I'll have to remember that.

I almost stepped on a rattlesnake yesterday! It was scary, but luckily I stopped just in time.

It's so beautiful in here. I've taken lots of pictures. I think if we had enough food, we could stay in here for weeks.

Oh yeah, I almost forgot. Our permit is only good for one night. Anyway, Zion is great. And so is this trip!

I'll write more soon. I promise!

Morgan

Saturday, July 22

This is James Parker reporting again.

I slept so good last night! I set up my tent in a sandy area about twenty feet away from the river. The sand was comfortable—and so was my air mattress. I was out like a light! And then when we woke up, it was like we were in the middle of a "Survivor" episode. We're camped in the middle of the Narrows. Well, not really. The map says the narrowest area starts right after Big Spring, which we'll pass this morning. That's almost hard to believe with all the Narrows we've already passed through. Anyway, I better go now. My parents' backpacks are nearly packed. And Morgan and I still need to filter water.

Yours,

James

Morgan dropped the hose into the river and held the pump. James took the other hose and placed it in the water bottle. Morgan pumped the handle and the bottle slowly filled with water.

"I'll pump this last one," James said to Morgan.

"Thanks," Morgan said. "My arm is getting tired."

Morgan and James finished filling up the water bottles. As they were packing up the filter, James looked up through the narrow canyon walls at the brightening sky. There were puffy white clouds overhead.

"We're ready to go," Morgan announced. She handed out the water bottles.

Maidenhair fern

The family headed downstream. They hiked in and out of the river, through rapids, small pools, and over slippery stones. At times, they walked on short trails along the side of the river.

Soon they came to a series of cascades pouring out of the cliffs.

"This must be Big Spring," James said.

"They said you can't miss it," Mom said. "And they sure were right."

The family put their packs down and crossed the river to get a closer look at Big Spring. The springs were surrounded by mosses, grasses, and maidenhair ferns.

"It's another hanging garden," Morgan said. She snapped several photos. Then the family drank from their water bottles and filtered more water from the fresher water at the spring.

When they returned to their packs, James pulled out his map. "From here on," he announced, "there's no more high ground. We're going into the deepest Narrows."

"Let's get a move on then," Dad said.

James took a step and slipped backward, landing on his pack. He got up, wet from the fall, but okay. A moment later, Mom slipped on a mossy rock and fell forward. But she stopped her fall with her hand and avoided plunging into the river.

"We need to be real careful," Mom said in a shaky voice. "It's awful slippery in here."

"And the current is strong," James added.

The family tromped through the water and crisscrossed back and forth, trying to find the safest parts of the river to walk in. Then they turned a corner and peered downstream at the dark canyon.

"Enter the most serious Narrows!" James announced.

The family trudged on.

"Nice step," Dad said to James as he carefully maneuvered around some boulders.

"There's a loose rock here," Morgan called out to her mom, who was right behind her.

"Watch out for this spot," James said. He stepped into a small rapid filled with mossy rocks.

"It's deep right here," Dad said. The water was up to his waist. "But follow me."

The family coached each other along the way. While they forged through the river, the sky had turned completely cloudy.

"I think I felt a drop of rain," Morgan said.

"I did too," Dad said.

They came to Orderville Canyon, a side canyon on the left. They

went over to the junction and looked up the small, narrow canyon with polished walls.

"Should we go up there?" James asked. "It looks pretty cool."

"Let's rest a minute and then decide," Mom said.

While eating some cheese, James looked up. "Hey! I just got hit by a raindrop too."

"So did I," Mom said.

"We'd better head on out now," Dad said. "Remember the weather report for today? There's an increasing chance of rain as the day goes on."

"But, Dad," James said, "can't we just explore up there a little ways?"

The rain started falling steadily.

"James," Mom said, "how far does the map say it is until the Riverside Walk?"

"It's about two more hours," James answered, looking at the map.

"We better go on, James," Mom said. "I'd like to go up and explore Orderville Canyon too. But remember how heavy it rained the other day? We can't be caught in here in a storm like that."

The family continued working their way down the river.

Dad took a step on a loose, slippery rock. He teetered and then tried to plant his walking stick and …

Dad's ankle gave way, and his legs went out from underneath him. His upper body crashed down with the weight of his heavy backpack. Dad's shoulder slammed into a boulder.

"Arggghhhh!" he screamed.

Morgan reached Dad first. "Dad! Are you okay?"

Dad lay still, half in the water and half out. The rushing water instantly soaked his backpack.

Mom and James hurried over.

Dad winced in pain. "Help me!"

"Where are you hurting?" Mom asked.

"My ankle and my shoulder," Dad said. "Here, grab my arms." He tried to hold them up. "Ahh! No, never mind." Dad quickly dropped his arms back down. "That won't work. My shoulder is killing me."

Dad slithered around in the water and loosened his pack from his back. "There, can you slide it off now?"

Dad turned sideways. Morgan slowly pulled off his backpack. Dad grimaced in pain. Morgan propped the pack up on some rocks.

"Okay," Dad said, "getting me out of here should be a bit easier now."

Mom, James, and Morgan helped stand Dad up. He put one arm around Mom's waist. He held his other arm across his stomach and kept it still. With Morgan and James holding him, Dad took one step and then another. Slowly, Dad limped out of the river. He made it onto the sand near some trees and turned around.

"Okay," Dad said, "hold onto me as I lower myself down."

Slowly, Dad sat down in the sand.

"Here, let me give you a pillow," James said. He gathered some clothes and towels and set them against a rock behind Dad's back. "You can lie back now," he said.

"Do you want us to get you into some dry clothes?" Mom asked.

"No. Not yet," Dad said. "Let's see how hurt I am. Can you take off my shoes? Gently?"

James quickly took the boot and sock off Dad's unhurt foot.

Morgan bent down and untied the laces on Dad's other shoe. She slowly pulled off his boot and sock.

Mom built up a raised area in the sand, and Dad propped his hurt foot on it.

"How does it look?" Dad asked.

"It's already swollen," Mom replied.

"I was afraid of that," Dad said. "I completely flipped my foot over on that last step."

"Do you think it's broken?" James asked.

"I don't know," Dad said. "It might only be a bad sprain. I've done this to it before, playing basketball. I don't know if I'll be able to walk out of here, though. I'm also worried about my shoulder."

"Your shoulder?" Mom asked.

"Yes," Dad replied. "When I fell over, it smashed against a rock. It's killing me."

"Let's take a look," Mom said.

Mom unbuttoned Dad's shirt.

"Ugh!" Dad said. He moved his hurt arm just enough to allow Mom to peel off his shirt.

"Does it hurt up here?" Mom asked. She pointed to a lump on top of Dad's shoulder.

"Yes. Right there."

"It looks like your bone is sticking up," James said.

"Great," Dad said. "I broke my shoulder in the Narrows."

A while later, Dad lay still in the sand. He was wearing dry clothes and was covered by a sleeping bag.

Light rain continued to fall. The canyon remained cool.

"What time do you think it is?" Dad asked.

"At least midafternoon," Mom replied.

"And you haven't seen any day hikers coming upstream?" Dad asked.

"I'll bet the weather is keeping them out," James said.

"Good point," Dad said. He slowly sat up. "We need to get out of here now."

"How?" Morgan asked.

"Help me up," Dad said.

James, Morgan, and Mom got behind Dad and helped prop him up. He gingerly took a step and winced in pain. He held onto Mom and took another step, and then another. "I guess I can walk," he said, "if you all help me. I just can't move my shoulder."

"But you can't walk in there!" Morgan said. She pointed toward the river. "And what if you fall again?"

"How are you even going to get your shoes on?" James asked.

"I don't know," Dad said. "Help me back down."

Dad hopped back to his place in the sand and slowly sat down. "Ayyy!" he cried out. "That hurts!" Dad took a deep breath and then said, "There's no way I can get out of here. Not with my shoulder and ankle like this."

The family moved Dad to higher ground as far away from the river as possible. Mom gave Dad some water to drink and a granola bar.

"Splitting up is the only option," Dad said. "I don't want all of us to spend a night in here, waiting to see if someone comes looking for us tomorrow."

"With the weather as it is, who knows if anyone will be heading up here?" Mom said. "Anyway, James and I can go get help. And Morgan, you can stay with Dad."

"Sounds like a plan," Dad said.

"Do you have all you need?" Morgan asked Mom and James.

"Yes," James said. "We left the filter, some food, and a tent with you. According to the map, it should be just over an hour until we hit the Riverside Walk."

There are many first-aid kits available for hiking or overnight trips. Some are extensive, with many supplies. Some are homemade, with a minimal amount of supplies. A bare-minimum first-aid kit should include:

Moleskin for blisters	Antibiotic ointment
Extra flashlight	Cleansing pads
Extra warm clothes	Gauze and bandages
Magnetic compass	Adhesive tape
Candles/matches	Safety pins
Pocketknife	Scissors
Aspirin/medication	Tweezers
Trowel and toilet paper	

"Don't forget where we are," Dad said.

"There's no way I wouldn't remember this exact spot," Mom said, looking around.

"If we hit Orderville Canyon when we come back, we'll know we've gone too far," James said.

"I love you," Mom said. She kissed Dad and Morgan and then stood up.

"We'll be back before you know it," James said.

"Just be careful!" Dad said. "We don't need another one of us getting hurt."

"We're going to be extremely careful," Mom promised.

She and James took off down the river. Morgan and Dad watched them disappear around a bend.

Morgan sat down next to her father. "Is there anything you need?" she asked.

"Not right now," Dad said. "As long as I don't move, it doesn't hurt too much."

"You sure?" Morgan asked.

Dad thought for a minute. "How about if you read to me?" he asked. "My book is in the top flap of my pack. It will be a good way to pass the time."

"Sure!" Morgan said.

After a while, Dad attempted to sit up. "Arrggh!" he complained. "Better get me some more ibuprofen, Morgan," he said, lying back down.

Morgan gave Dad two pills and some water.

"It's a good thing you're here to help," Dad said. "How does the weather look?"

Morgan scooted toward the river and looked up. "It's still cloudy. But it's only sprinkling."

"That's good," Dad said. "We'd have nowhere to go if the water level rose."

"Are you warm enough?" Morgan asked.

"Yes," Dad said. "The sleeping bag is keeping me warm."

▲ ▼ ▲ ▼ ▲ ▼ ▲ ▼ ▲ ▼ ▲ ▼ ▲ ▼

James and Mom trudged downstream. A light rain continued to fall.

James kept looking around to see if the water level appeared to be rising. He was worried about a flash flood. "I think we're lucky," James said. "It isn't raining that hard."

"I'll consider us even luckier when we get Dad out of here safely!" Mom said. "But you're right. So far, we aren't getting a big thunderstorm."

Mom and James trekked on. The canyon opened up and it got brighter. They passed a small waterfall cascading down a cliff.

"It sure is pretty in here," Mom commented.

"Please keep watching your step," James reminded Mom.

"I am," Mom said. She reached out and touched James's shoulder. "Thanks."

Mom and James looked downstream. About a hundred feet away were rock steps leading up out of the Narrows.

"Mom, I think it's the end of the trail!" James called out.

They walked forward quickly. Two people appeared at the top of the stairs.

"Help! Down here!" James shouted. He and Mom splashed forward.

The couple walked down the stairs to meet them.

"My father's hurt back there," James said. "He can't walk!"

"How far back?" the man asked.

"About a mile, near Orderville Canyon," Mom answered. "We need to get a rescue crew."

"The best thing to do is get you to the bus," the man said. "They should be able to call a ranger for you."

"You're right," Mom said.

"Are you two okay?" the woman asked. "Do you need any water or food?"

"No, I think we can make it," James answered.

"But thanks for offering," Mom said.

FLASH FLOODS

Flash floods in Zion's canyons do happen, and they can be very dangerous. Hiking permits are not issued if the speed of the flowing water is greater than 120 cubic centimeters per second. In 1966, the water level in the Narrows quickly went from 200 cubic centimeters per second to 9,000 cubic centimeters per second. This huge flood of water had the power to push rocks the size of cars. Hikers in the Narrows could not survive this type of flood.

In general, canyon hikers should always get the latest weather reports before heading out. If bad weather threatens, hikers should stay out of a narrow canyon. Also, hikers should watch for worsening weather conditions, water turning muddy, and floating debris. If these things happen, the hiker should get to high ground immediately and stay there until conditions improve.

Mom and James walked quickly on the Riverside Walk. It was a mile to the end of the road where buses dropped people off to hike.

Morgan stepped out of the tent she'd just set up.

Drops of rain pattered down steadily. "There. It's all ready for you now," she said to Dad.

"Thanks," Dad said. "Now I just have to get in."

"Let me know how I can help," Morgan said.

"I will," Dad replied. He sat up slowly. "Man, this hurts!" he exclaimed. Using his good arm, Dad scooted himself backward until he reached the door of the tent. Morgan pressed the mattress down, and Dad slithered inside. He lay back on the pillow Morgan had arranged for him.

"Ahh, relief!" Dad said. "That wasn't easy."

Morgan covered her father with the sleeping bag. "I'm going to go filter some water before dark," Morgan said. "Then I'll get our lantern ready."

"Good thinking," Dad said. "It looks like we may be here all night."

"Well, I sure hope Mom and James made it out okay," Morgan said.

▲ ▼ ▲ ▼ ▲ ▼ ▲ ▼ ▲ ▼ ▲ ▼

Mom and James flagged down a bus driver. They told the driver about the accident, and he radioed for help. Mom and James sat under the shelter at the bus stop waiting for a rescue team.

"It's getting dark," James said.

"Good thing we left most of our food and the water filter with Morgan and Dad," Mom said.

"And two flashlights," James added.

A patrol car drove up. Its windshield wipers slapped back and forth. Mom and James jumped up.

The ranger rolled down the window. "Are you the party in need of assistance?"

"Yes!" James said. "My dad's hurt in the Narrows."

The ranger got out of the car and asked Mom and James some questions. She wanted to know exactly where Dad was and how serious his injuries appeared to be. She also wanted to know how Dad was being treated and if he had any food, water, or shelter.

Mom and James answered the ranger's questions and explained that Morgan had stayed back to help Dad.

"That's great," the ranger said. "Then I think we'll send in a medic tonight, and the rescue team will go get him first thing in the morning."

▲ ▼ ▲ ▼ ▲ ▼ ▲ ▼ ▲ ▼ ▲ ▼ ▲ ▼

Morgan closed the book she was reading to Dad. "What time do you think it is?" she asked.

"I don't know," Dad said. "How dark is it?"

"I'll go check," Morgan said. She climbed out of the tent. She turned her flashlight on and carefully walked toward the river and looked up. It was so dark, it was hard to tell where the canyon walls ended and the sky began. Raindrops continued to patter down. Morgan walked back toward the tent and peered inside.

"It's completely dark," she said.

"It's got to be at least ten o'clock then," Dad said. "How's the weather?"

"Still raining," Morgan answered, "but only lightly."

"And the river?" Dad asked.

"It's hard to tell," Morgan said. "It sounds loud. But I'm not sure if it's because it's nighttime and quiet out or if the water level is rising."

▲ ▼ ▲ ▼ ▲ ▼ ▲ ▼ ▲ ▼ ▲ ▼ ▲ ▼

The ranger drove Mom and James back to the campground.

"I wish we could have gone in there with the medic," James said.

"It's much better this way," the ranger said. "Our medic is used to the Narrows and walking in there at night. He can go twice as fast this way. Besides, we wouldn't want to take the chance of anyone else getting hurt."

"What do we do now?" Mom asked.

"I don't think there's much you can do," the ranger replied. "It's best for the two of you to try and get some rest. You've had a rough day."

The ranger stopped at the family's campsite. "Okay," she said, "we'll see you first thing in the morning."

"Okay," James said.

Mom and James got out of the car and looked around.

"The rain stopped," James said.

They sat on the bench at the picnic table.

"It sure is lonely out here without Morgan and Dad," James said.

"I know," Mom said, "but why don't we try to get some sleep."

▲ ▼ ▲ ▼ ▲ ▼ ▲ ▼ ▲ ▼ ▲ ▼ ▲ ▼

Morgan lay back and stared at the top of the tent. She listened to Dad's breathing. He seemed to be asleep. Then Morgan saw a flash of light against the tent.

"Anybody hurt up there?" someone called out.

"Over here!" Morgan shouted. She climbed out of the tent and waved her flashlight back and forth.

The medic scrambled over to Morgan. "Where's your father?"

"In here," Morgan said.

"Who's out there?" Dad asked.

The medic peered into the tent. "Where are you hurt, sir?"

"My shoulder and my leg," Dad replied.

The medic asked Dad a few questions. Then he gave him some pain medication and started treating his injuries.

"Is he going to be okay?" Morgan asked.

"I think so," the medic answered. "But we'll know a whole lot more when we get him out of here tomorrow."

Early in the morning a group of rescuers found Morgan, Dad, and the medic.

"How's he feeling?" one of the rescuers asked.

"Stabilized," the medic replied. "We've got some pain medication in him. He's a bit weak and groggy. But we should be able to get him out of here now."

The crew used a flat board to get Dad out of the tent and onto a rescue raft. They secured him down while Morgan packed up all the supplies and put them away in their packs.

"And how about you?" a rescuer asked Morgan. "Are you able to walk out?"

"You bet," Morgan said.

The rescuer took Morgan's backpack and slung it on his back. "You'll be able to walk faster this way," he said to Morgan. Another ranger grabbed Dad's pack.

The crew lifted the rescue raft and carried it to the water.

"I never thought I'd go through the Narrows this way," Dad said.

"Me neither," Morgan agreed, grabbing her walking stick. She followed the rescuers. "It sure is easier walking without a pack on."

"Thanks for all your help, Morgan," Dad said. "You've been great."

▲ ▼ ▲ ▼ ▲ ▼ ▲ ▼ ▲ ▼ ▲ ▼

James and Mom waited at the top of the rock steps at the end of the Narrows. Below them on the gravel was a wheeled litter, a rescue vehicle that would be used to wheel Dad back to an ambulance.

"Did you get much sleep last night?" the ranger asked.

"No," James answered, "I couldn't stop thinking about Dad and Morgan."

"I can understand that," the ranger said. "But they should be here soon. And at least the weather is cooperating."

James looked up at the clear sky.

"Look!" Mom called out. "There they are!"

The team carrying Dad in the rescue raft had just turned the last bend in the river. Morgan was right next to them, plodding along with her walking stick.

"Dad! Morgan!" James called out.

Dad opened his eyes, lifted his good arm, and waved.

"Hey!" Morgan called out. "We're all right!"

James and Mom hurried down the steps. The rescuers were already pulling Dad's raft out of the river.

"Long time, no see," Dad said from the rescue raft.

"How are you?" Mom asked. She touched her husband's forehead.

"I've never been better," Dad joked. "Well, actually, not that good. I'm looking forward to getting to a doctor."

"How about you, Morgan?" James asked.

"Good," Morgan said, "now that I know Dad's going to be all right."

James took the change from the cashier at the lodge gift shop. "I'm going to put this poster of the Narrows up in my bedroom," he announced.

"Me too," Morgan said. She held up her poster.

"Here, help me out," Dad said.

It was two days later and Dad's left ankle was wrapped in an Ace bandage. His right arm was in a sling. He put his left arm on James's shoulder and slowly walked out of the gift shop. "I'll catch up with you at the bus stop," he said.

"We'll wait for you," Morgan said.

The family slowly walked with Dad.

As Dad limped along, he noticed an older woman sitting on a bench reading a book. Her left leg was in a cast and propped up on a wheel-chair in front of her. Dad walked toward the woman, thinking that something about her looked familiar.

"Where are you going?" James asked Dad.

"Just a second," Dad said, hobbling toward the woman.

Dad got within a few feet of the woman. "Hi," he said. Mom, James, and Morgan came up beside him. "Remember us?"

The woman stopped reading and shielded her eyes from the sun. She paused for a second. "Yes, I do!" she said, smiling. "You're the family who rescued me at Bryce."

The Virgin River in Zion Canyon

"Well, not quite, Colleen," Morgan said. "But we were glad to help."

Colleen looked at Dad. "What happened to you?"

"Probably about the same thing that happened to you," Dad said. "I fell while hiking in the Narrows. How are you feeling?"

"Better than a few days ago," Colleen answered.

"Shouldn't you be at home, resting?" James asked.

"Not at all!" Colleen said, laughing. "While in the hospital, I already wanted to be back outside." She gestured to Dad. "Here, have a seat."

Dad sat down next to Colleen.

"My sister came to get me," Colleen went on. "But then I realized after getting released that all I'm going to do at home is sit around until I get well. And I thought, you know, I could do that just as well in a national park. Besides, what's a visit to Bryce without going to Zion too?"

James smiled. "That's just what our parents said."

"It must be hard coming to a place like this and not being able to do anything, though," Morgan said.

"Well, you're right," Colleen replied. "But I've been here at the lodge for a few days now. And I realized that, as much as I like to hike, there's so much to see right here. Do you know we had a group of deer grazing on the lawn last evening? And then a bunch of wild turkeys showed up," Colleen went on. "And look at the scenery!" She swept her arm across the horizon. "I've got the best view in the world!"

"Still, I envy you," Colleen said. "I haven't been in the Narrows for years. I was hoping to get back there on this trip. Now I don't know when I'll get to go." She gestured toward the cast on her leg. "Things like this don't heal quickly when you're my age."

"The Narrows is a beautiful place," Mom said, "but it is not an easy hike."

"I can see that," Colleen said, looking at Dad. "But was it worth it?"

"Oh, yes," Dad said. "I plan on bringing all of us there again soon. I want to see what I missed."

"I wanted to get my sister to wheel me out on the Riverside Walk," Colleen said. "It's paved and accessible to wheelchairs. But it's just too much for her. There are some small hills on the trail."

For a moment, it was quiet.

Then Morgan spoke. "You know," she said, "we could help wheel you out there."

Again it got quiet. Mom looked at Dad. James looked at Morgan. Then Morgan and James looked at their parents.

Colleen looked at all of them. "I wouldn't want to put you through any trouble. In my own way, I'm quite content right here. I've got this great book, and … "

"Do you think you're up for it?" Mom asked Dad.

"Up for it?" Dad said. "Of course I am! I'll hobble along at my own pace."

A woman came out of the gift shop and walked toward Colleen. "Hey, here comes my sister," Colleen said.

"Kathleen, this is the family that rescued me," Colleen told the woman. Colleen introduced Kathleen to the family.

"It's nice to meet you, Kathleen," Dad said. "We were wondering if you and Colleen would like to join us on a hike? We're willing to help you with Colleen's wheelchair."

Kathleen thought for a second. "That sounds nice," she said. She looked at her sister. "Get back in your wheelchair. I know how much you want to see the park."

"Let's go!" James said. He got behind Colleen's wheelchair and helped guide her to the bus stop. The group of six took the next bus toward the Temple of Sinawava and the Riverside Walk—one more time.

Date: Tuesday, July 25

Dear Diary,

Well, we are on the way back home now. But so much has happened, I don't know where to start.

We did hike through the Narrows, but it didn't turn out as planned. Dad got hurt and I had to spend the night out there with him. Then we had a rescue team come get him. It was pretty scary, but he's doing much better now.

I'm so sad about leaving this place. And I was sad to leave Bryce too. We got to see so much! Dad says we're going to come back to both parks sometime and see parts of the park we didn't get a chance to see this time. But between now and then, at least I'll have my pictures to look at. Anyway, I have to say good-bye now to you, Zion.

Until next time,

Morgan

Date: Tuesday, July 25

This is James Parker reporting. I'm happy to say my dad is already recovering and should be back to full strength within a few months. He had a fall in the Narrows and hurt his ankle and shoulder. Dad says we're coming back sometime to see some of the places we missed. I've been looking at the maps of both parks. I think we should try hiking to Kolob Arch, Taylor Creek, and the Fairyland and Riggs Springs Loop Trails at Bryce. Anyway, all in all, it's been a great trip, and we're all sorry to have to go home.

Until next summer,

James

JAMES AND MORGAN'S TOP TEN LIST

(SUGGESTIONS OF THING TO SEE AND DO IN ZION AND BRYCE)

BRYCE

1. Navajo Loop Trail
2. Queen's Garden Trail
3. Peekaboo Trail
4. Night Sky Program
5. The Rim Trail between Sunrise and Sunset Points
6. Riggs Springs/Bristlecone Loop Trails
7. Under-the-Rim Trail for Backpacking
8. The Visitor Center
9. Junior Ranger Program
10. Fairyland Loop Trail

I'll never forget the rocks
at Bryce, or the sunset!

ZION

ZION
NATIONAL
PARK
U.S. DEPARTMENT OF THE INTERIOR
NATIONAL PARK SERVICE
NATIONAL
PARK
SERVICE
Department
of the Interior